Stallion by Starlight

Magic Tree House® Books

#1: Dinosaurs Before Dark
#2: The Knight at Dawn
#3: Mummies in the Morning
#4: Pirates Past Noon
#5: Night of the Ninjas
#6: Afternoon on the Amazon
#7: Sunset of the Sabertooth
#8: Midnight on the Moon
#9: Dolphins at Daybreak
#10: Ghost Town at Sundown
#11: Lions at Lunchtime
#12: Polar Bears Past Bedtime
#13: Vacation Under the Volcano
#14: Day of the Dragon King
#15: Viking Ships at Sunrise
#16: Hour of the Olympics
#17: Tonight on the *Titanic*
#18: Buffalo Before Breakfast
#19: Tigers at Twilight
#20: Dingoes at Dinnertime
#21: Civil War on Sunday
#22: Revolutionary War on Wednesday
#23: Twister on Tuesday
#24: Earthquake in the Early Morning
#25: Stage Fright on a Summer Night
#26: Good Morning, Gorillas
#27: Thanksgiving on Thursday
#28: High Tide in Hawaii

Merlin Missions

#29: Christmas in Camelot
#30: Haunted Castle on Hallows Eve
#31: Summer of the Sea Serpent
#32: Winter of the Ice Wizard
#33: Carnival at Candlelight
#34: Season of the Sandstorms
#35: Night of the New Magicians
#36: Blizzard of the Blue Moon
#37: Dragon of the Red Dawn
#38: Monday with a Mad Genius
#39: Dark Day in the Deep Sea
#40: Eve of the Emperor Penguin
#41: Moonlight on the Magic Flute
#42: A Good Night for Ghosts

#43: Leprechaun in Late Winter
#44: A Ghost Tale for Christmas Time
#45: A Crazy Day with Cobras
#46: Dogs in the Dead of Night
#47: Abe Lincoln at Last!
#48: A Perfect Time for Pandas

Magic Tree House® Fact Trackers

Dinosaurs
Knights and Castles
Mummies and Pyramids
Pirates
Rain Forests
Space
Titanic
Twisters and Other Terrible Storms
Dolphins and Sharks
Ancient Greece and the Olympics
American Revolution
Sabertooths and the Ice Age
Pilgrims
Ancient Rome and Pompeii
Tsunamis and Other Natural Disasters
Polar Bears and the Arctic
Sea Monsters
Penguins and Antarctica
Leonardo da Vinci
Ghosts
Leprechauns and Irish Folklore
Rags and Riches: Kids in the Time of Charles Dickens
Snakes and Other Reptiles
Dog Heroes
Abraham Lincoln
Pandas and Other Endangered Species
Horse Heroes

NEW!

More Magic Tree House®

Games and Puzzles from the Tree House

MAGIC TREE HOUSE® #49
A MERLIN MISSION

Stallion by Starlight

by Mary Pope Osborne

illustrated by Sal Murdocca

A STEPPING STONE BOOK™

Random House New York

Text copyright © 2013 by Mary Pope Osborne
Jacket art and interior illustrations copyright © 2013 by Sal Murdocca

All rights reserved. Published in the United States by Random House Children's Books, a division of Random House, Inc., New York.

Random House and the colophon are registered trademarks and A Stepping Stone Book and the colophon are trademarks of Random House, Inc. Magic Tree House is a registered trademark of Mary Pope Osborne; used under license.

Visit us on the Web!
randomhouse.com/kids
MagicTreeHouse.com

Educators and librarians, for a variety of teaching tools, visit us at
RHTeachersLibrarians.com

Library of Congress Cataloging-in-Publication Data
Osborne, Mary Pope.
Stallion by starlight / by Mary Pope Osborne ; illustrated by Sal Murdocca.
  p. cm. — (Magic tree house ; #49)
Summary: Jack and Annie are magically transported to Ancient Greece to find the meaning of greatness. There they meet the young Alexander the Great and take part in the famous story of how he tamed his horse, Bucephalus.
ISBN 978-0-307-98040-3 (trade) — ISBN 978-0-307-98042-7 (lib. bdg.) —
ISBN 978-0-307-98043-4 (ebook)
[1. Magic—Fiction. 2. Time travel—Fiction. 3. Brothers and sisters—Fiction.
4. Horses—Fiction. 5. Alexander, the Great, 356–323 B.C.—Fiction.]
I. Murdocca, Sal, ill. II. Title.
PZ7.O81167Ssl 2013 [Fic]—dc23 2012020525

Printed in the United States of America
10 9 8 7 6 5 4 3 2 1
First Edition

To Phoenix Valentine van Rhyn

CONTENTS

Prologue   1

1. The Ring of Truth   3

2. Keep Walking   13

3. Big Thinkers   25

4. The One-Eyed King   36

5. The Race   46

6. Warhorses   57

7. Stallion at Starlight   68

8. Night Riders   81

9. The Truth   90

10. A Place of Honor   100

    Author's Note   109

    Excerpt from *Horse Heroes* 111

Prologue

One summer day in Frog Creek, Pennsylvania, a mysterious tree house appeared in the woods. It was filled with books. A boy named Jack and his sister, Annie, found the tree house and soon discovered that it was magic. They could go to any time and place in history just by pointing to a picture in one of the books. While they were gone, no time at all passed back in Frog Creek.

Jack and Annie eventually found out that the tree house belonged to Morgan le Fay, a magical librarian from the legendary realm of Camelot. They have since traveled on many adventures in the magic tree house and completed many missions for both Morgan le Fay and her friend

Merlin the magician. Teddy and Kathleen, two young enchanters from Camelot, have sometimes helped Jack and Annie in both big and small ways.

Jack and Annie are about to find out what their next magic tree house mission will be!

CHAPTER ONE

The Ring of Truth

"I love looking at your notebook," Annie said. "It helps me remember all of our adventures." She turned a few pages. "Aww, polar bears in the Arctic. The cubs were so cute . . . and Pompeii and the volcano! Oh my gosh, remember Hercules?"

"Yep," said Jack without looking up.

It was a warm day in June. Jack and Annie were sitting on the front porch of their house. While Annie thumbed through his notebook, Jack was reading a book about giant pandas in China.

"Ooh," said Annie as she flipped through more pages. "The ghost town in the Wild West! The invisible piano player, remember?"

"Yep."

Annie turned another page. "Remember Australia? The baby kangaroo, the koala, the dingoes! The forest fire!"

Jack looked up. "Yep," he said. "Look, that's all cool, but I can't talk now. I'm trying to read the last page of my book."

"You're going to need a new notebook soon. This one is almost full." Annie closed the notebook and put it into Jack's backpack. She stretched. "I think I'll go for a bike ride," she said. "Maybe stop by the library . . . go to the pool."

Jack closed his book. "Done!" he said. "Now I need something new to read. I'll ride to the library with you." As he pulled on his backpack, Jack caught sight of something out of the corner of his eye. He turned, and what he saw was incredible.

A small penguin was standing on the sidewalk in front of their house.

"Penny?" Jack said.

"Oh!" cried Annie. "Oh! Oh! Oh!" She dashed off the porch.

Jack ran after Annie. They both knelt down beside the little penguin. "What are *you* doing here?" Annie asked.

Jack picked Penny up, and he and Annie stroked the penguin's downy head. "Hey, what's happening, Penny?" he said. "Why are you here?"

Peep.

"The tree house!" said Annie. "It must be back."

"Hey, guys!" Jack and Annie's dad called from behind the screen door of their porch.

Annie quickly jumped in front of Jack to hide the little penguin. "What is it, Dad?" she said.

"I just made some fresh lemonade," their dad said.

"Thanks!" Annie said. "We'll have some as soon as we come back!"

"We're heading into the woods for a few minutes!" said Jack.

"Okay. It'll be in the fridge," their dad said.

5

"Thanks," said Jack. "See you later!"

"Let's go!" said Annie.

Holding Penny in his arms, Jack hurried with Annie down the sidewalk. "Did you come here with Teddy and Kathleen?" he asked the penguin.

Peep.

"Is that yes or no?" asked Jack.

Peep.

"Yes," Jack said.

"No," said Annie at the same time.

"I guess we'll soon find out," said Jack.

Jack and Annie crossed the quiet street and headed into the Frog Creek woods. As they hurried through the dappled light, the air smelled of summer. Squirrels scurried up trees. Crows cawed to one another.

When Jack and Annie came to the tallest oak, they stopped. The tree house was nestled in the branches near the top. A long rope ladder dangled down to the ground.

"Teddy! Kathleen!" shouted Annie.

There was no answer.

Peep.

"So you came here all by yourself?" Jack said to Penny. "Is something wrong in Camelot? Are Teddy and Kathleen okay? What about Morgan and Merlin?"

"Let's go!" said Annie. She started up the rope ladder. Still holding the little penguin, Jack awkwardly climbed after her.

"Oh, wow!" said Annie when she reached the tree house.

"Oh, wow *what*?" asked Jack. He hoisted Penny into the tree house and climbed in after her. Then he also whispered *"Oh, wow."*

An old man with a long white beard, a pointed hat covered in stars, and a red cloak stood in a shadowy corner.

"Merlin!" breathed Annie.

"I see Penny found you," the master magician of Camelot said in his velvety voice. The little penguin waddled to Merlin and stood beside him.

"Yes," said Jack. "She came right up to our house."

"Is something wrong in Camelot?" asked Annie.

"No, all is fine," said Merlin. "Your friends are well. I just decided I wanted to visit you myself."

"Cool," said Jack shyly. Merlin had never come to Frog Creek all by himself.

"Let me tell you what is on my mind," said Merlin. "I have been thinking very deep thoughts, pondering questions that wise men and women have pondered through the ages."

"Pondering?" asked Annie.

"*Ponder* means to think carefully about a subject," Jack said. "Right?" he asked Merlin.

"Exactly," said Merlin. "I have been pondering questions about life. For instance, I have been wondering about the idea of *greatness*. What are the secrets of greatness? What makes a person truly great?"

"That *is* a good question," said Jack.

"I cannot answer it by myself, as I do not live in your world—the world of time and mortals," said Merlin. "So, on each of your next four missions, you will meet someone who will help you learn a true secret of greatness."

"That sounds like fun," said Annie.

"I hope it will be," said Merlin. "To begin, how would you like to meet someone called Alexander the Great?"

"Oh, man, I've heard of him!" said Jack.

"I haven't," said Annie, "but he sounds . . . well, great."

Merlin smiled.

"Can I ask a question?" Jack said.

"Of course," said Merlin.

"To be practical, how will we know when we've found a secret of greatness?" Jack asked.

"I pondered that as well," said Merlin. "I have brought something magical to help you." The magician reached into his cloak and pulled out a small gold ring. "I call this the Ring of Truth."

"The Ring of Truth," Annie repeated.

"I have cast a spell on the ring," said Merlin. "Wear it on your journeys. When you discover a true secret of greatness, the ring will glow."

"May I wear it?" Annie asked Merlin. He nodded. Annie held out her hand, and the magician slipped the gold band onto her finger.

"I have brought another bit of magic as well," said Merlin. He reached into his cloak again, and this time, he pulled out a tiny glass bottle. Silver mist swirled inside of it.

"Mist gathered at first light on the first day of the new moon on the Isle of Avalon," said Merlin.

"Wow," said Annie.

"The magical mist will allow you to experience greatness in *yourselves*," said Merlin. "When you need help, make a wish to have an extraordinary talent. Then breathe in the scent of the mist, and for one hour that talent will be yours. The magic will work only once on each journey."

"Thanks!" said Jack. He took the bottle from Merlin and put it into his backpack.

"And finally, Morgan asked me to give you a research book." The magician reached into his cloak for a third time and pulled out a book.

"I've never heard of Macedonia," said Jack.

"It is the kingdom where Alexander was born," said Merlin. "The ancient Macedonians are fierce and warlike, so travel cautiously."

Fierce? Warlike? Jack wanted to hear more.

Merlin picked Penny up and raised his hand in farewell. "Go now," he said. "Good luck."

"Bye, Merlin. Bye, Penny," said Annie.

Peep.

"Wait—" began Jack.

But before Jack could ask another question, Merlin and Penny vanished.

"Let's go," said Annie. She pointed at the cover of the book. "I wish we could go there!" she said.

The wind started to blow.

The tree house started to spin.

It spun faster and faster.

Then everything was still.

Absolutely still.

CHAPTER TWO

Keep Walking

Jack and Annie were wearing tunics with soft belts and lace-up sandals. A cloth bag had replaced Jack's backpack. He looked into the bag and saw his notebook, his pencil, and the bottle with the magic mist from the Isle of Avalon.

"We wore clothes like these when we went to Pompeii," said Annie.

"Yeah, and when we went to the Greek Olympic Games," said Jack.

"When *you* went to the games," said Annie. "They didn't let girls in, remember?"

"Oh, right," said Jack. "You nearly caused a riot when you tried to sneak in."

"It wasn't my fault," said Annie.

Jack and Annie looked out the window together. The air felt dry and hot. The sun was directly overhead in a cloudless sky. The tree house was low to the ground, tucked into the spreading branches of an olive tree. Donkeys and horses ambled up a winding dirt road.

"This looks like a quiet, sleepy place," said Annie, "not fierce or warlike at all."

"I wonder what Merlin meant," said Jack. He opened their book to the first page and read out loud:

> More than 2,300 years ago, Macedonia was a kingdom north of Greece. It was ruled by King Philip II, the father of Alexander the Great. The brilliant and ferocious king was known far and wide for his military skills.

"Ferocious king," Jack repeated. "Well, I guess that fits."

"Don't worry, we have magic that gives us a great talent," said Annie. "So we can wish to have military skills, too."

"I can't picture us having military skills," said Jack.

"Come on, let's go look for Alexander the Great!" said Annie. She started down the rope ladder. Jack packed up the book and followed her.

Several men on donkeys were riding by on the

dirt road. Annie started to call out to them.

"Don't," Jack whispered, stopping her. "People might ask us questions we can't answer."

"But I only wanted to ask them where Alexander the Great lives," said Annie.

"Let's just try to blend in first," said Jack, "until we know our way around."

Annie sighed, but she kept quiet as she and Jack followed the donkeys up the dusty road. They passed rocky meadows dotted with cows, and small farmhouses with tiled roofs, chickens, and vineyards. They saw a shepherd tending sheep, a goat herder herding goats, and a farmer with a plow pulled by an ox.

"Can we ask someone now?" Annie said.

"Let's wait," said Jack. "We don't want to draw attention to ourselves unless we have to."

They kept walking. Soon they rounded some tall rocks. Beyond a stone wall was a huge field. Thousands of warriors were marching.

"Yikes," said Annie. She and Jack stopped and stared at the warriors.

"That must be the king's army!" said Jack.

The foot soldiers wore armor and helmets with tall crests. In one hand, each man carried an oval shield. In the other hand, each held a long, pointed spear. Behind the foot soldiers were rows of soldiers on horses.

"They're just practicing, right?" said Annie.

"I hope so," said Jack. "I don't see any enemies." He pulled out the research book and found a chapter called "The King's Army." He read aloud:

At the time of King Philip II, Macedonia was threatened on all sides, by frontier tribes as well as the Persian army. King Philip II drilled his men night and day, until his army became the best fighting machine in the known world.

Jack looked at the soldiers again. They marched to the right and then the left. The front row of soldiers pointed their spears forward. The other rows pointed their spears up in the air. All the men moved in perfect unison, their helmets, shields, and spears flashing in the sunlight.

"They *do* look like a fighting machine," said Annie.

Jack thought they looked more like a monstrous insect with thousands of legs and spikes sticking out of its body. He shivered. "Let's get away from this place," he said.

Jack and Annie headed farther up the dusty road. Finally, beyond a grove of olive trees, they came to a walled town. Above the town a white mansion sat on a hilltop.

"Maybe that's where King Philip the Second of Macedonia and Alexander the Great live," said Annie, pointing at the mansion.

Jack and Annie walked through the town gate and headed toward a market square. On the street leading to the square, a group of boys were sword-fighting with sticks. "Hello—" Annie called.

"Don't," said Jack.

It was too late. The boys stopped fighting and stared at them.

"Does King Philip of Macedonia live on that hill?" Annie asked, pointing to the columned house.

The boys scowled at Annie.

Jack grabbed Annie's arm and pulled her along. "Keep walking," he said under his breath. "Turn right."

"Thanks anyway!" Annie called. She and Jack kept going and turned right at the next corner. "They weren't very friendly," said Annie.

"No kidding," said Jack. "Listen, do *not* draw attention to yourself. These are fierce and warlike people with a ferocious king."

"They were just kids," Annie protested.

"Doesn't matter. Keep your head down. Act cool," said Jack.

"I am cool!" said Annie. "*You* act cool."

Jack and Annie walked toward the bright market square, which was filled with carts and tents. Bordering the square was a covered walkway.

"Want to walk over there so we can be in the shade?" said Jack, pointing. The hot sunlight was starting to get to him.

"Sure," said Annie.

They headed over to the covered walkway. It was lined with shops, where men made and sold pottery, jewelry, and weapons.

Jack stopped to watch some blacksmiths. "I wonder what they're making," he said. One of the blacksmiths used tongs to lift a piece of red-hot metal from a fire. Another hammered the metal into a curved shape.

"Whoa, it's a sword," said Jack. He pulled out his notebook and pencil. He opened the notebook and wrote:

sword makers heat iron, hammer with

Before Jack could finish his thought, Annie poked him. "Watch it, you're drawing attention to yourself!" she whispered.

"What?" Jack looked up.

The blacksmiths were glaring at him.

"Maybe they think you're stealing military secrets," said Annie.

"Uh-oh," said Jack. "Let's go." Clutching his notebook, he hurried down the covered walkway. Annie followed him.

Jack looked over her shoulder. "They're following!"

"That way!" said Annie. She grabbed Jack's arm and pulled him back into the crowded sunlit square. The two of them walked faster and faster, weaving around food stalls that sold stuffed grape leaves, eggs, fish, cheese, and bread.

Annie glanced back. "They're still searching for us!"

The blacksmiths were standing in the crowd, looking around. "We've got to hide!" Jack said.

"Where?" said Annie.

"I don't know! Duck down!" said Jack.

Ducking their heads, they passed a group of teenage boys gathered under a canopy. The boys were listening quietly to a man with a curly beard.

"Here! Here!" said Jack. He pulled Annie under the canopy, and they stood with the group.

The boys were all taking notes on wooden

tablets covered with wax. They used pieces of bone
to carve words into the wax.

"Act like you're a student," Jack whispered to
Annie.

As the teacher lectured to the group, Jack pre-
tended to take notes in his notebook.

"As you all know, the earth is the center of the universe," the man said in an easy, calm voice.

"He's wrong," Annie whispered to Jack.

"Shh," Jack whispered. "In ancient times, everyone thought that." He glanced out at the square and saw the blacksmiths passing by. When they were out of sight, he whispered to Annie, "Let's go, quick, before they come back."

Annie didn't budge. She was listening carefully to the teacher. "The sun and planets revolve around the earth," the man said.

"That's *totally* wrong," Annie whispered to Jack.

"Who cares?" said Jack. "We have to go. We have to—"

"But we can't let him teach something *wrong*," said Annie.

"Forget it," said Jack. "We—"

Before Jack could finish, Annie raised her hand. "Excuse me!" she called out. "The earth is *not* the center of the universe!"

CHAPTER THREE

Big Thinkers

"Ha-ha," Jack laughed, as if Annie were crazy. "Don't pay attention to her. We're leaving now."

"Who are you to defy our teacher?" a boy shouted.

"How dare a *girl* insult him!" another yelled. He shook his fist at Annie.

"She wasn't insulting anyone," said Jack. "But don't worry, we're going." He took Annie's arm and started to pull her along.

"Stay!" the teacher commanded.

Jack and Annie froze.

"Tell me more," the man said. "It is rare that I am surprised—and you have surprised me. What do you mean, the earth is not the center of the universe?"

"Well," said Annie, "the earth is a planet, and all the planets in our solar system travel around the sun."

The teacher smiled. "Is that what you believe?" he said.

"It's not just what I *believe.* It's what I *know,*" said Annie. "A trip around the sun takes a year."

The students laughed. "You are speaking nonsense," one said. "And wasting our precious time with Aristotle!"

Aristotle? thought Jack. He knew that name. His mind raced, trying to remember who Aristotle was.

"I'm just telling you the facts," said Annie. "While the earth is circling the sun, it rotates. *Rotate* means it spins around. One rotation of the earth is one day."

The boys snickered, but Aristotle was quiet.

"What a novel idea," he said softly. Then he turned to the boys. "Our class is over for the day. I would like to speak to these two visitors alone."

The boys grumbled, but they tucked their tablets under their arms and headed out into the bright square.

Aristotle stared at Jack and Annie. "Who are you? Where are you from?" he asked.

"I'm Annie. This is Jack, my brother. And, um, we're from Frog Creek."

"Frog Creek . . . ?" said Aristotle.

"It's west of Greece," Jack said.

"And who are *you*?" asked Annie.

"My name is Aristotle. I have come from Athens, Greece, to teach philosophy and science in Macedonia."

Jack gasped. Now he remembered! Aristotle was a great philosopher and scientist in ancient Greece! On a past mission, they had delivered his writings to the ruler of Baghdad.

"We've heard of you," said Annie. "You're a big thinker. We saved your writings once, but a camel ate them." She laughed. "It wasn't funny at the time. But—"

"*Annie,*" said Jack. He shook his head. It would be impossible to explain their trip to Baghdad. That trip had happened more than a thousand years after *this* time in history. "My sister has a big imagination," he said.

"So it would seem," said Aristotle. "Her ideas about the universe are completely wrong, of course, but I am astonished that she has a theory."

"Why?" asked Annie.

"I did not think that girls had the ability to think about such things," said Aristotle.

Annie looked at Jack. "He's kidding, right?" she said.

Jack laughed nervously. "Well, no," he said. "That's what people thought a long time ago."

Scowling, Annie started to say something, but Aristotle smiled at her. "You must be a very special kind of girl. Come. Let us walk and talk, and you can show me what big thinkers you both are."

Jack and Annie fell into step with the philosopher as he started across the square. "Besides contemplating the universe, what else do you think about?" Aristotle asked Annie.

"Um . . . I think a lot about animals," she said.

"Wonderful. Animals always reveal to us something natural and beautiful," said Aristotle. "So you study them?"

"I *do* study them," Annie said. "But more than that, I fall in love with them. I think that's the way I really learn."

"Ah, very good," said Aristotle. "To truly educate your mind, you must also educate your heart. And where does your heart lead you, Jack? Do you prefer a life of sports? Military training?"

Jack shook his head. "I'm not super-great at sports," he said, "or military training. But I'm good at doing research. I take notes on everything." Jack found it surprisingly easy to talk with the philosopher. "I love learning about the rain forests and the deep sea and the moon. I love learning about everything, really."

"Me too!" said Annie.

"Indeed?" said Aristotle. "You both are re-markable!"

Jack shrugged. "Not really. I guess we just kind of know ourselves."

"So it would seem," Aristotle said. "Knowing yourself is the beginning of all wisdom."

"The more Jack and I learn about the world, the more we learn about ourselves," said Annie. "We're always trying new stuff."

"Yeah, even if we make fools of ourselves some-times," said Jack. "Especially me."

Aristotle chuckled. "I think we should all dare to make fools of ourselves again and again," he said. "Anyone who fears looking like a fool must say nothing, do nothing, and be nothing."

"So it would seem," said Annie.

"May I ask: why have you come to Macedonia?" said Aristotle. "Does your visit have a purpose?"

"It does," said Jack with a laugh. He was en-joying talking to Aristotle so much that he'd forgotten their mission. "Actually, we're looking for Alexander the Great."

"Do you know him?" asked Annie.

"I know a prince named Alexander, the son of King Philip," said Aristotle.

"That's him!" said Annie.

"But I must say, I would not call him *great* yet," said Aristotle. "He is only twelve years old."

"Twelve?" said Jack.

"Yes. Alexander is the reason I, too, have come to Macedonia," said Aristotle. "When the prince turns thirteen in a few weeks, I will become his tutor. Why are you looking for him?"

"We'd love to spend some time with him," said Annie. "We heard he was . . . you know, great."

Aristotle sighed. "The prince would certainly wish you to think so," he said. "Well. If you want to meet him, King Philip is having a gathering at the Royal House this afternoon. It is close by." Aristotle pointed to the mansion on the hill above the square. "The prince will be in attendance. Would you like to go with me?"

"Yes!" Jack and Annie said together.

"Good. Then let us climb the hill," said the

philosopher, and he started up a pebble path that led to the Royal House.

Jack and Annie followed, grinning at each other. "This is fantastic!" Jack said softly. "Maybe our mission will be easier than I thought!"

When they reached the top of the hill, Jack was surprised by the plainness of the Royal House. It looked like a big white box with a tiled roof and simple columns. Two guards in crested helmets stood like statues by the entrance. Each held a giant shield decorated with a star.

"Please wait outside," said Aristotle. "I must alert the king that I have brought guests to his gathering—and that one of them is a girl."

"Why?" asked Annie. "No girls allowed?"

"I fear females are never allowed to attend such events," said Aristotle. "But I imagine the king has never met a girl like you before."

"Thanks," said Annie. "I think." After Aristotle left, she turned to Jack. "What is *wrong* with all the men in history? Nearly everywhere we go in

the tree house, girls aren't allowed to do any of the
fun stuff."

"I know, it's crazy," said Jack. "But stay calm.
Remember, the king's a ferocious fighter."

"Yeah, well . . ." Annie held up her fists. "We have magic that could make *me* a great fighter, too," she said.

"Don't even think about it," said Jack, glancing at the guards.

Annie lowered her fists. "Aren't you surprised that Alexander's only twelve?" she said. "At home he'd be just a sixth or seventh grader."

"I know. How great can he be?" said Jack. He pulled out their book and looked up *Alexander, childhood* in the index. With his back to the guards, Jack read in a soft voice:

Young Alexander was raised in the manner of noble youths. From an early age, he received military training and became an excellent swordsman, spear thrower, and chariot driver. He was a champion athlete and excelled in all sports.

"Oh, man," said Jack. "He sounds like Superman."

"Aristotle's back," whispered Annie.

Jack slipped the book into his bag.

"The king has granted his permission," Aristotle said, looking at Annie. "You may *both* come inside."

"Hurray!" said Annie. Then she and Jack followed the philosopher into the Royal House.

CHAPTER FOUR

The One-Eyed King

The front hallway was dark and cool. The flickering flames of oil lamps cast shadows on wall murals. The murals showed figures from Greek myths.

"Zeus," Annie whispered to Jack, pointing to a painting of the ruler of all the Greek gods.

"Centaurs," whispered Jack, pointing to creatures that were half man and half horse.

"This way," said Aristotle.

Jack and Annie followed the philosopher through the hall to an open courtyard. Women in long white dresses were grilling meat over a fire and pulling bread from a clay oven. They glanced at Annie with curiosity.

Aristotle led them past the cooks to a doorway off the courtyard. The sounds of loud conversation came from the room beyond.

"King Philip has gathered the men of his most elite cavalry," said Aristotle. "They are known as the King's Companions. Do not be startled when you look upon the king. Years ago, he lost an eye in battle."

"Oww," said Annie, wincing.

"Even so, he is still the greatest military leader in the known world," said Aristotle.

Jack nodded. He took a deep breath.

"Prince Alexander will be arriving soon," said the philosopher. "Come." Then he led Jack and Annie into the spacious, lamp-lit room.

The King's Companions lay on couches, propped up on their elbows, or on pillows. They were talking and eating. King Philip was on a couch draped in purple silk. He had a black patch over one eye. Two bodyguards with curved swords hanging from their belts stood nearby.

When the king and his men caught sight of Jack and Annie and Aristotle, they fell silent.

"King Philip the Second of Macedonia," Aristotle said, bowing.

Jack and Annie bowed also.

"I have just met these two very learned young people today," said Aristotle. "They are Jack and his sister, Annie, of Frog Creek, a land west of Greece."

"Hi," said Annie with a smile.

Jack smiled, too, as he looked around at the warriors.

No one smiled back, including King Philip II of Macedonia. "Sit," the king ordered.

Jack and Annie sat together on an empty couch. Aristotle sat nearby. Three servants quickly appeared. The King's Companions resumed eating and talking as a servant removed Jack's sandals. She rinsed his dust-covered feet in a tub of warm water. Jack kept his eyes down, not sure what to do or say.

Next, servants delivered small dishes of food to them. Jack identified olives, cheese, purple grapes, nuts, figs . . . and then there was something that looked like dead bugs.

Annie caught Jack's eye. "Grasshoppers?" she whispered, wrinkling her nose.

"Eat the grapes," he whispered back.

Jack and Annie silently ate grapes as the King's Companions feasted and talked with Aristotle and King Philip. The king was telling a story about a stallion that had been taken captive.

Not until the dishes were cleared away did King Philip turn his gaze on Jack and Annie. "Silence!" the king ordered his men. "It is time now to hear from our esteemed visitors. Whomever Aristotle admires, I admire also."

Jack nearly choked on a grape.

"Aristotle tells us you have studied and learned much—both of you," the king said, looking at Annie. "Is that true?"

Before Annie could answer, a boy burst into the room. He was fair-haired and muscular. He wore a purple cloak over his tunic. He strode to the center of the room, tossed back his cloak, and bowed.

"I greet you all!" the boy declared. "At last I have arrived!"

"Hail, Prince Alexander!" the men said in unison.

Alexander the Great! Jack thought.

Prince Alexander started to speak, but to Jack's surprise, the king snapped at him, "Quiet, boy! Sit down!"

The smile left the prince's face, but he obeyed and sat on a couch near his father.

Aristotle leaned forward and spoke kindly to Alexander. "My prince," he said, "when you en-

tered, we were about to hear from two learned young people from Frog Creek, a land west of Greece. They have come here expressly to meet *you*. This is Jack and his sister, Annie."

"I see," said Alexander, puffing out his chest. He gave Jack and Annie a superior smile. "Well then, small visitors, please share with us your great knowledge."

Is this kid serious? Jack wondered. *Who does he think he is?*

"I'll share," Annie piped up. "Recently we

learned a lot about a rare kind of bear called a panda bear."

"Panda bear?" said the prince with a smirk.

"Yes, but don't confuse pandas with other bears, like polar bears or grizzly bears," said Annie. "Pandas live in China. Polar bears live in the Arctic."

"That's right," said Jack, clearing his throat. "They're very heavy, polar bears, but they can move over thin sheets of ice. They balance their weight and slide on their paws."

"Like this," said Annie. She held out her arms and moved as if she were sliding over ice. She laughed—and the king and his companions laughed with her.

"How wondrous!" the king exclaimed to Aristotle.

"Yes, indeed," said the philosopher.

The prince, though, looked bored.

"And then there are koala bears," said Jack.

"Enough about bears!" Alexander said rudely. "Let us talk about the lion hunt I recently went on."

"Not now!" the king snapped. He looked at Jack. "I want to hear more about the bears."

Jack cleared his throat. "Actually, koala bears are not *bears* at all," he said. He was eager to show off his knowledge in front of the prince. "They're marsupials. A kangaroo is a marsupial, too."

"Kang-a-roos?" Alexander said in a mocking voice. *"Mar-soop-eels?"*

"Kangaroos are as tall as a person," said Annie, "but they hop like frogs. They can box, too. Like this . . ." Facing Alexander, she punched the air with her fists.

The prince automatically ducked, making the King's Companions laugh. The king laughed loudest.

"How foolish she is!" the prince growled.

"Quiet, Alexander, do not be angry," said his father. "Go on, tell us more," he said to Jack and Annie. "Do you honor the Greek gods as we do?"

"I'm not sure what you mean by *honor*," said Annie. "But we actually met Hercules in Pompeii. Pegasus saved us at the Greek Olympics. They're favorites of ours."

The men looked confused. *"What?"* said the king.

"What I mean," Annie said quickly, "is that we believe in the power of the imagination and the power of ancient stories. By reading about Hercules and Pegasus, we feel like we know them."

"Right. And they're constellations," said Jack. "So if you look at the stars in the night sky, you'll see that the old stories are always with us. We are never alone."

Jack glanced around the room. The king and his companions were smiling and nodding. Only the prince looked unhappy.

"Thank you, Jack. Those are wise words," said Aristotle.

"Yes, indeed," said the king. "Aristotle, your young friends are truly amazing. Alexander, you would do well to learn from these two."

"Learn *what*?" Alexander asked. "Can this boy mount a chariot moving at full speed? Can he throw a spear farther than a grown man? Can he hunt a lion?"

"No, and he never will," Annie said. She smiled at the prince. "But Jack's great at writing. He takes notes and he writes his own stories."

"Ah . . . ah!" said Alexander. He sprang to his feet. "Forgive my rudeness," he said to Jack. "I would like to talk with you alone. Perhaps you *can* help me."

Uh-oh, thought Jack.

The prince looked at his father. "May we go?"

Please say no, thought Jack. Alexander made him nervous.

But King Philip nodded. "We hate to lose your company," he said to Jack, "but it would be good for you to counsel my son."

"Yes, indeed. Come with me, small visitors from Frog Creek," said Alexander, beckoning to Jack and Annie.

Jack glanced at Aristotle.

The philosopher looked nervous, too, but he smiled encouragingly and nodded, as if to say, *Be brave. Dare again to make fools of yourselves.*

CHAPTER FIVE

The Race

As they followed Alexander, Jack wished he hadn't shown off. What if the prince challenged him to mount a moving chariot? Or hunt a lion? As he followed Alexander out of the room, Annie hurried along with him.

Prince Alexander strode ahead through the courtyard. He led Jack and Annie to a covered porch behind the house.

"So, what would you like us to do for you?" asked Annie, smiling.

Alexander gazed down at her. "Well, I would

like a girl to do nothing for me," he said. "You should be with the other females, cooking and spinning."

The smile left Annie's face. "Fine," she said. "I'll go back in and hang out with Aristotle." She started back through the door.

"I'll go, too," said Jack, eager to get away from the arrogant prince.

"Halt!" barked Alexander. He looked at Annie. "I will endure you awhile longer. You boast that your brother likes to write things down? Well, now he has something very important to write about: me! Do you have something to write with?" he asked Jack.

"Sure." Jack pulled out his notebook and pencil.

"When you return to your own country, your writing could bring me lasting fame there," said Alexander.

"You bet," said Jack. Writing was easy, he thought. Mounting a moving chariot wasn't.

"We will walk and talk," the prince ordered.

"Come." Jack and Annie followed Alexander off the porch, stepping into the hot sunlight.

The prince led them through a garden overlooking the hillside. On a plateau near the bottom of the slope was a long barn with a riding ring.

"You said Hercules is a favorite hero of yours," the prince said. "Did you know he is my great-great-grandfather?"

"Who? Hercules?" asked Annie.

"Yes. And since he is a son of Zeus, I am a living Greek god myself," said Alexander.

Whoa, thought Jack. He rolled his eyes.

"You mock me?" Alexander asked.

"No, no, I just got some dust in my eyes," said Jack. He rubbed his eyes.

"A living Greek god," said Annie. "Write that down, Jack."

"Of course," said Jack. But he wrote:

This guy's a raving nut.

Annie read Jack's notes and snickered.

Alexander turned and looked at her.

Annie tried to change her snicker into a snort. "Sorry, got some dust up my nose," she said, scratching her nose.

The prince kept walking and talking. "This means, of course, that when I go to war, I will never lose a battle. Soon I will be master of the universe."

"Cool," said Jack. But he wrote:

This guy should be locked up.

Annie glanced at Jack's notes and stifled a laugh. Alexander looked at her again.

"Dust in my throat," she said. She coughed.

Alexander kept walking. "You said you went to the Olympics in Greece?" he said. "Well, so have I."

"Were you competing?" said Jack.

"Of course not. I never compete with other athletes," the prince said wearily. "I would win every time. I am the greatest living athlete in the world."

"Amazing," said Jack. But he wrote:

What a show-off! He could never have
friends.

Jack looked up. "More?" he said.

"First I would like to see all you have written so far," said the prince.

"You would?" said Jack, gulping.

"Yes."

"Uh—but I'm not finished," said Jack. "I don't like to show my writing until I've gotten all my notes together." He closed his notebook and started to put it in his bag.

"I want to read it *now*," said the prince, snatching the notebook. He opened it and looked at Jack's notes. "'A raving nut'? What is that?"

"Um . . . in our land, a 'raving nut' is a very rare and valuable kind of nut," said Jack.

"Right, by comparing you to a raving nut, Jack's saying you are very valuable," added Annie.

Alexander looked at Annie suspiciously, then back at the notebook. "'This guy should be locked up,'" he read.

"For protection!" said Annie. "Someone as great as you should be locked up for your own safety. You're a living Greek god, for goodness' sake!"

Alexander read more: "'What a show-off!'" He looked puzzled. "Show-off?" he asked.

"That means you can't help showing the world how great you are," said Jack.

"Ah, that is true," said Alexander. The prince then read Jack's last note: "'He could never have friends.'" For a second, the prince looked hurt.

"That—uh—I mean it must be really hard for you to find people who are as great as you to hang out with . . . ," Jack said lamely.

"Hmm," said Alexander. He closed the notebook and handed it back to Jack. "Perhaps we should compare athletic skills now," he said.

"Your skills with mine?" said Jack.

"Don't you want to tell us more about yourself?" Annie asked the prince.

"No, I want to learn more about Jack," said Alexander. "Let us race one another," he said to Jack. He pointed down the hill. "To the stable fence and back."

"I'd rather not," said Jack.

"You must race me! Now!" the prince ordered.

"Okay, okay," said Jack. He was a pretty good runner. Maybe he had a chance to win. He put away his pencil and notebook and handed his bag to Annie. Then he knelt down on one knee.

"GO!" shouted Alexander.

The prince sprinted down the hill toward the stable, his purple cloak flying behind him. Jack ran as fast as he could, but Prince Alexander ran much faster.

By the time Jack touched the fence of the stable, Alexander was already running back up the hill. In the searing heat of the late afternoon, Jack struggled to keep going. Halfway up the hill, he felt like he might pass out.

"Come on, Jack! Come on!" yelled Annie.

Alexander stood at the top of the hill, grinning down at him.

When Jack finally reached Alexander and Annie, he wobbled a few steps and collapsed.

"Jack!" Annie cried. She knelt beside him. "Are you okay?"

Alexander walked over to them. Instead of helping Jack up, he just stared down at him. "I think being a winner is much better than being a friend," the prince said. "Don't you?"

"No!" said Annie. "You're mean."

"All right. I'll give your brother another chance," said Alexander. "Would you like to race again, Jack? Or perhaps wrestle?"

Jack didn't answer. He was just trying to breathe.

"I didn't think so," said Alexander. "Perhaps you should compete against girls in the future."

"Very funny," Annie said. "Hold on, Prince." She reached into Jack's bag and pulled out the tiny bottle. Then she leaned close to Jack and whispered in his ear, "Here, sniff the magic mist.

Race him again. Show him!" She slipped the tiny bottle into Jack's hand.

Jack wrapped his fingers around the bottle. All he had to do was sniff and make a wish to be the greatest athlete in the world. He clutched the bottle tighter.

Then a strange calm came over Jack. He *could* use Merlin's magic. But he didn't really want to. Or need to. Why waste it on a mean, arrogant bully?

"No, I don't want to race you again," Jack said. Even though he felt sick, he forced himself to sit up. "You're clearly a much better athlete than I am."

The sound of hoofbeats came from the stable below. Men were herding horses into the fenced-in riding ring. Alexander let out a whoop. Without glancing back, he ran down the hill.

Jack and Annie watched the prince climb the fence and join the men and horses in the ring. In the distance, accompanied by his bodyguards and companions, King Philip was heading down to the stable, too.

"You sure you're okay?" Annie asked Jack.

"I'm fine," he said, though he still felt woozy from the heat. "Here, put this back." He handed the bottle to Annie. "He's not worth it."

"You're right," said Annie.

"I'm totally done with him," said Jack.

"What about our mission?" Annie asked. "There's a truth about greatness we're supposed to learn from him. And we haven't learned it yet."

"Yes, we have," said Jack. "The truth is: he's not that great."

Annie held up her finger to show Jack the ring. "I don't think that's it. The Ring of Truth isn't glowing."

"I don't care," Jack said slowly. "I never want to see him again. I don't trust him. I don't like him. And I certainly don't need to learn anything from him."

CHAPTER SIX

Warhorses

Annie sighed. "I agree with you. But what are we going to do?"

"I don't know." Jack dropped his head into his hands. His skull was pounding. He felt like he might throw up.

"Do you want to leave Macedonia?" asked Annie.

"No," said Jack, shaking his head.

"You want to stay?" Annie said.

"No," said Jack.

"Jack! Annie!" someone shouted.

Jack lifted his head. Aristotle was striding toward them. When he reached them, he looked at Jack and said, "You need water. Come with me."

Annie helped Jack to his feet. Jack still felt wobbly as they followed Aristotle to a well near the Royal House. He and Annie splashed water from a bucket onto their faces and drank from their cupped hands. The cool, clear water made Jack feel better. "Thank you," he said.

"Did the prince make a proper fool of you?" Aristotle asked Jack.

"More or less," said Jack.

"Ah, you are not the only one," Aristotle said. "It's because he so greatly fears looking like a fool himself. He is desperate to equal his father's power and strength."

"Well, someone needs to remind him he's only twelve," said Annie.

Aristotle smiled. "I agree. Where is he now?"

"He ran to see the horses," said Annie.

"Ah, yes," said Aristotle, peering down the hill. "The King's Companions are all eager to see the warhorses a seller has brought from Thessaly. Would you like to see them, too?"

"I love horses," said Annie. "But . . ." She looked at Jack.

"You guys go. I'll wait here," he said. He didn't want to be anywhere near Prince Alexander.

"I don't want to leave you," said Annie. "Please come with us. Please."

Jack stared at her and then sighed. "Okay," he said.

As Aristotle, Jack, and Annie started down the hill, the sun was low in the sky. Jack was silent as Annie chatted with Aristotle. "So do warhorses go to war?" she asked.

Aristotle nodded. "They carry soldiers to war in lands near and far," he said. "Their speed and strength can help save a man's life or win a battle."

"What a hard job," said Annie.

"Yes, but they are the most honored horses in the kingdom," said Aristotle.

When Jack, Annie, and Aristotle reached the riding ring, the horses were all standing in a row with grooms attending them. As the King's Companions watched from outside the fence, King Philip and the small, wiry horse seller walked together down the line, discussing each animal. Alexander walked behind them, looking in the horses' mouths and feeling their legs.

"The prince loves horses, too," Aristotle said.

Too bad for the horses, Jack thought.

"What are they looking for?" Annie asked.

"Thick bones, strong teeth, and a good bend in the knees," said Aristotle, "a broad chest and high-set neck, bony head, large nostrils, a thick mane, small ears."

"That's a lot," Annie said.

The king came to the end of the line and began to haggle with the horse seller. Alexander tried to be part of the conversation, but his father silenced him. Jack almost felt sorry for the prince. King Philip pointed to a couple of horses. The horse seller nodded, and then the grooms led all the horses from the riding ring back into the barn.

The setting sun flashed over the hillside. "The

horse trading is over for today," said Aristotle. "It will resume at daylight tomorrow."

Suddenly a black stallion bolted from the barn. Several grooms ran after him. The stallion was stunningly beautiful. As he trotted around the ring, the light of the setting sun seemed to set his dark coat and mane on fire. He held his head high and arched his neck. He had small ears and wide eyes.

"That must be the magnificent horse I have heard so much about," said Aristotle.

"Who is he?" asked Annie.

"His name is Bucephalus," said Aristotle. "He once belonged to the Royal Horse Master of Thessaly."

When the stallion slowed to a walk, a groom approached him and tried to grab his bridle. But as the man's shadow fell over Bucephalus, the stallion neighed and bucked. He broke away from the man and backed against the fence. His ears were flat against his head. His eyes were wild.

"What's going on?" said Annie.

"He was once a noble warhorse," said Aristotle. "But ever since he was captured in battle, he has not let any rider mount him."

"Why?" asked Annie.

"No one knows," said Aristotle. "But the seller insists he can be tamed again and wants a bag of gold for him."

A groom threw a rope around the horse's neck. Another brought out a whip.

"What's that for?" asked Annie.

The groom cracked the whip on the ground.

"No!" shouted Prince Alexander. "Put the whip down!"

The groom cracked the whip again. The horse reared up. Arching his neck, he kicked his hooves, almost trampling the man who held the whip. The grooms jumped back to avoid being crushed.

"No!" shouted Alexander again, rushing forward. "Do not hit him!" He grabbed the whip from the groom and threw it to the ground.

"Do not be a fool!" the king roared at the prince. "Let them do their job!"

Alexander ignored his father. He walked calmly toward the stallion. The horse stared at him for a moment, then took off across the ring. Alexander started running after him.

"Stop him!" the king ordered his bodyguards. Two of the guards rushed forward and grabbed Alexander before he reached the horse. They held the prince as more grooms approached Bucephalus. The stallion reared up again.

"This horse cannot be tamed!" the king shouted at the horse seller.

"Yes he can!" shouted Alexander. He tried to break free from the guards, but they held him tightly. "And I am the one who can tame him!"

"Take him from my sight! He is worthless!" shouted the king. Jack couldn't tell if the king meant the stallion or the prince.

The grooms drove the black stallion back into the stable. And the guards held on to Alexander as they followed the king and his companions back up the hill. Several times, the king turned and shouted at his son: "You fool!" "So reckless!" "Arrogant!"

"Excuse me," said Aristotle. "I must try to calm the king." He strode away, leaving Jack and Annie alone.

"Boy, Alexander's dad is really mean to him," said Annie.

"I noticed that at the house," said Jack. "He kept telling Alexander to be quiet."

Jack and Annie were quiet themselves as they watched King Philip yell at the prince all the way back to the Royal House. By the time the king and his party had gone inside, the sun had slipped behind the hill. Night was falling fast. The air had grown cooler.

"I know we think Alexander's a mean kid and a show-off," said Annie, "but just now he was trying to protect the black stallion."

Jack didn't say anything.

"And we were kind of mean to him, too, actually," said Annie. "We made fun of him and stuff. We did."

"He deserved it," Jack mumbled.

"But the truth is we were showing off a little, too," said Annie, "to the king and his men."

"Fine. So what's your point?" Jack said, sighing.

"Probably we're even," said Annie. "Maybe we should start over with him."

"Oh, brother," said Jack, but he actually agreed with her. Strangely, his anger at the prince had faded. He even felt sorry for him now.

"I think his life is pretty sad," said Annie. "Maybe we could help him somehow."

"How do you help a kid like that?" said Jack.

"I don't know," said Annie.

"Well, let's start with a question," said Jack. "What do we know about him so far?"

"We know he craves excellence and glory," said Annie. "That's what Aristotle told us."

"We know he's desperate to equal his father's power and strength," said Annie.

"And he thinks he's the great-great-grandson of Hercules," said Jack.

"Right. He's a living Greek god," Annie said.

"And the world's greatest athlete," said Jack.

"And soon he'll be master of the universe," said Annie.

Annie laughed, and Jack laughed with her. "He's ridiculous," Jack said, shaking his head.

"I've never met a kid like him before," said Annie.

"Thank goodness!" said Jack.

"But we also know something else about him," said Annie.

"What?" said Jack.

"We know he loves Bucephalus," Annie said.

"Yeah . . . so?" said Jack.

"So let's start there," said Annie. "Love is always a good place to start. Don't you think?"

CHAPTER SEVEN

Stallion at Starlight

Jack stared at Annie for a moment. "So . . . what do you have in mind?" he said.

"We could try to train Bucephalus for Alexander," said Annie. "Then maybe his dad would let him keep the horse."

"Are you serious?" said Jack. "You and me train him?"

"We've done it before," said Annie. "Remember when we went to the Wild West and helped save the mustangs? We learned some rules on how to treat a horse."

"That journey was a long time ago," said Jack.

"But you took notes," said Annie. "I saw them in your notebook today."

"Yeah, well, we might have notes, but we don't have much experience," said Jack. "We weren't there long enough."

"Let's just look at your notes," said Annie.

Jack pulled out his notebook and found the notes he'd taken during their adventure in the Wild West. "Horse rules," he read aloud. "Soft hand, firm voice, sunny attitude, praise, reward."

"Simple. We just have to be nice and kind and positive," said Annie. "Let's try it." She started toward the gate.

"Are you crazy? There's lots more to it than that," said Jack, following her. "Those guys in the ring have tons of experience! And they couldn't do anything with that horse!"

"Forget those guys," said Annie. "We're a million times nicer to animals than they are. And I have a sunny attitude." She opened the gate and started across the long stretch of grass to the stable.

"But that horse is dangerous, Annie," Jack said as he followed her to the stable entrance. "Don't just think you can tame him!"

"Now you sound like King Philip," said Annie. "Let's find the horse first, then we'll figure out what to do."

Jack and Annie peeked into the shadowy stable. It smelled of wood, barley, and hay. Contented sounds of snuffling, snorting, and munching came from the stalls. From the other end of the barn, though, came neighing and stamping noises.

"I think he's at the far end," said Annie. She looked around. "I don't think anyone's in here now. Let's look."

"Move fast!" said Jack. They stepped into the dark stable. Jack grabbed a lamp from a wooden table. The flickering light cast strange shadows as he and Annie moved past the stalls toward the end of the barn.

Jack held the lamp high as they passed a white horse, several brown horses, and a brown-and-white spotted horse. Bucephalus was in the very last stall.

His coat shone in the lamplight. He was completely black, except for a white star on his forehead. His eyes still had a wild look, and his ears were flattened against the sides of his head. Jack thought he looked angry.

"Hi, Bucephalus," Annie said in a warm, friendly voice. "Boy, are we happy to see you. And I know you're happy to see us, too!"

"No he isn't," Jack said. "This isn't going to work."

But Annie lifted the latch on the door and calmly stepped inside, closing the door behind her.

"Don't worry, Jack. I have a way with animals, remember?" said Annie. She jumped onto a bale of hay and put her leg over the horse's back.

"No! No! You don't just climb on—" said Jack.

The stallion gave a loud snort, then kicked his back hooves and dropped his head down, trying to buck Annie off.

"Whoa!" cried Annie, clutching the horse's mane.

The horse hurled himself against the door. Jack barely got out of the way before the animal shot out of the stall. With Annie clinging to his mane, the horse ran through the long barn and out the open doorway!

"Stop!" Jack shouted. He blew out the lamp and ran after the stallion and Annie.

Outside in the riding ring, the horse reared. Annie was holding on with all her might. The stallion loomed above Jack, raking the air with his front hooves. Jack could see the whites of his eyes.

Jack stumbled backward and fell. At the same time, Annie tumbled off the horse. The stallion galloped across the grassy ring.

Jack scrambled over to Annie. "You okay?" he cried.

"Yes!" She sat up. "You were right . . . being nice wasn't enough . . . ," she said, trying to catch her breath. "I made a fool of myself. . . . I guess I don't have enough experience."

The stallion stopped near the fence. He stood against the purple-blue sky of early evening, snorting loudly.

"Don't feel bad," said Jack. "It would take tons of experience to train a horse like him."

"Well . . ." Annie was still struggling to breathe. "We . . . you know we could be great horse trainers if we really wanted to."

"What do you mean?" asked Jack.

"The . . . the magic," Annie said. "We sniff the magic mist and then . . . then make a wish to become great horse trainers."

"But does this have anything to do with our mission?" Jack said. "If it doesn't, it wouldn't be practical to use our magic now."

"It might not be practical," said Annie, "but I feel like it's the right thing to do."

Jack looked at the stallion. The animal made a soft blowing sound. He stared intensely back at Jack, as if trying to tell him something. "Okay," said Jack, surprising himself. "I guess we could give it a try. Why not?"

"Great!" said Annie. "This is going to be so much fun!" She jumped to her feet.

"Slow down," said Jack, standing up. He reached into his bag and pulled out the tiny glass bottle. The silver mist from the Isle of Avalon swirled inside. "So here's what we do—we make a wish to be two great horse trainers."

"Yes!" said Annie.

"Okay," said Jack. "I wonder what happens when you're the greatest horse trainers ever."

"We'll soon find out," said Annie.

Jack lifted the bottle into the air. "We wish to be two great horse trainers!" Then he uncorked the bottle, closed his eyes, and deeply inhaled the magic mist.

A mix of wonderful smells overcame him: sweet honeysuckle with damp summer grass and leaves in sunshine.

When Jack opened his eyes, he felt light-headed. He held the bottle out to Annie, and she inhaled the mist, too. "Ahhhh," she breathed.

Jack corked the tiny bottle and put it away. He and Annie grinned at each other. "All set?" Annie asked.

"You bet," said Jack. He wasn't worried now. He felt as calm and relaxed as if he had tamed a thousand wild stallions.

"Hello, Buddy," Annie said to the stallion. "Do you mind if we just call you Buddy? It's much easier than Bucephalus."

Jack laughed quietly. Buddy *was* a better name.

Buddy pricked his ears as if he were listening to her. "Do you mind if we come closer, Buddy?" Annie asked.

The horse didn't move.

Annie started walking very slowly toward him. Jack walked with her. When they were close enough to touch him, Buddy backed up nervously. He swished his tail and arched his neck.

"It's okay, Buddy," Jack said in a soft voice. "It's okay, it's okay." Jack concentrated on the stallion. He poured all his energy, all his compassion, and all his strength into the horse . . . until he felt that he and Buddy were one and the same creature.

DO NOT COME CLOSE.

"What?" Jack said, looking around. Was he hearing the horse's thoughts?

"You don't want us to come close to you, Buddy?" Annie asked.

Oh, man, thought Jack. *Annie heard him, too. This must be what happens when you're a really great horse trainer: you understand what horses are thinking!*

Jack looked deeply into the stallion's eyes. He tried to hear the horse's thoughts again.

DO NOT COME CLOSER.

"Okay, we won't," Jack said, keeping his voice calm and soothing. "We won't come closer until you are ready."

"That's right," said Annie. "But tell us, why can't we come close?"

NO RIDERS.

"Why no riders?" Jack asked the horse. "You once had riders, didn't you?"

"We won't hurt you, Buddy," said Annie. "We promise."

Buddy lowered his head.

LOST.

"You're lost?" said Annie.

LOST.

Jack remembered what Aristotle had told them. "He used to belong to the Royal Horse Master of Thessaly," he said to Annie. He looked into the horse's eyes again. "Is it your master?" he asked the stallion. "Is your master lost?"

The horse threw back his head and sniffed the air.

Jack and Annie were quiet for a moment. Then Annie said softly, "I'm afraid your master is not coming back. Not ever."

The horse was still.

"Do you miss him?" Annie asked.

The stallion tossed his head. Jack thought he heard a word.

SAD.

The stallion's sadness washed over Jack, filling him with sorrow, too. "I'm sorry," he said.

"We're really sorry," said Annie. She sounded like she might cry.

Jack took another step toward the horse. Annie stepped with him. This time, the stallion didn't back away.

Annie breathed on the horse's muzzle so he could smell her breath. Jack did the same. Then Annie touched the stallion's forehead, and Jack touched him, too. Annie moved her hand down the horse's nose, while Jack stroked the horse's long neck. The animal's velvety coat smelled of grass and wind.

"Just know this," Jack said to the stallion. He spoke tenderly and with all his heart. "Whatever happened to your master was not your fault. Not at all."

The stallion lowered his head and nuzzled Jack and Annie. His whole body shuddered, as if he were sighing with relief.

CHAPTER EIGHT

Night Riders

Stars twinkled in the night sky. Jack and Annie were quiet for a long time. Then Annie gently rubbed the horse's neck and said, "Hey, Buddy, let's go for a ride. Want to?"

The stallion stood very still for a moment. Jack wondered if the horse understood. But then he raised his head.

YES.

"Great. You go first," Annie said to Jack.

Jack grabbed a handful of the horse's mane. Buddy didn't move. He didn't snort or balk. Jack took a couple of short steps and pushed off the ground. As if he had springs on his feet, he gracefully vaulted onto the horse's back.

Jack reached out his hand. Annie took it. Then, as smoothly as a gymnast, she pushed off the ground and leapt onto the horse's back behind Jack.

Jack and Annie settled comfortably into place, balancing themselves. Jack felt as if he'd lived on the back of a stallion all his life. He grabbed Buddy's mane again and held on tightly. He gripped with his legs and leaned forward and whispered, "Let's go."

The stallion stamped the ground. Then he started walking slowly forward. Jack and Annie moved in perfect rhythm with his step. When they came to the gate of the riding ring, Jack pushed it open with his foot.

The stallion pranced out of the ring. Soon his hooves were crunching lightly over the pebble path leading down to the square. The town was quiet under a blanket of stars. Market stalls had shut down for the night. Merchants, craftsmen, and shoppers had gone home.

When the stallion reached the square, a warm wind urged him forward. He quickened his gait and began to trot. Jack and Annie moved in time with his steps: one-two, one-two, one-two.

The stallion picked up speed, until he began to canter. Jack and Annie moved in time to a different, smoother rhythm: one-two-three, one-two-three. Jack felt as if they were all dancing together.

When the stallion came to the wide road that led from the square, he began to gallop. He took long, swinging strides, until his hooves barely touched the ground.

Jack had the feeling that his legs had become one with the horse's legs, his breath had become one with the horse's breath, his skin had become one with the horse's skin.

Buddy ran on, unafraid of the dark. He galloped along the dirt road, passing the moonlit military field where the king's army was still drilling for war.

The stallion kept galloping. He passed meadows where sheep and cows slept under the stars. He passed quiet farmhouses and barking dogs.

As Buddy galloped lightly over the country-side, Jack and Annie knew how to sit evenly and how to breathe deeply. They knew when to lean forward and when to shift their weight back. If they wanted Buddy to slow down or speed up or turn, they only had to shift their bodies slightly, and the horse seemed to understand.

Buddy soon left the road and started over a grassy field. Jack couldn't see what was ahead, but he trusted the horse's instincts. He trusted his own, too. He felt completely safe.

When Buddy jumped over narrow ravines, Jack knew how to relax his body and cling to the horse's mane. When Buddy splashed through swamps and marshes, Jack knew how to stay centered on the horse's back.

All through the night, Jack, Annie, and Buddy traveled over the countryside. When the horse finally slowed down to a steady walk, Jack began to grow sleepy. He rested his head on Buddy's neck.

Jack heard frogs croaking in the wet reeds and crickets chirping in the dry grass. His body rocked as Buddy's hooves tapped over the hard, cracked earth, through olive groves and rocky fields. He closed his eyes. . . .

"Jack." Annie nudged him from behind.

"What?" Jack asked in a daze.

"Wake up."

"What?" Jack opened his eyes.

The sun was up. In the rosy dawn, Buddy was ambling along the wide dirt road that led back to town. Sheep had risen to their feet and were grazing on dewy grass. A cool breeze blew by Jack's face. It smelled of open fields and damp woolly lambs.

"Guess what?" said Annie. "Our hour was up a long time ago."

"What do you mean?" said Jack, sitting up straight.

"The magic hour, when we were great horse trainers," said Annie.

"What about it?" said Jack.

"It ended," said Annie. "For a long time, we've been riding Buddy just as ourselves."

"Really?" Jack said. "The magic ended?"

"Don't worry," said Annie. "Buddy doesn't mind riders now. We helped him understand that we're his friends, and that it's okay to let other people ride him. He's not waiting for his master anymore."

"Oh, wow," Jack said softly. He stroked Buddy's damp neck. "Thank you for the great ride."

The stallion whinnied and kept trotting. Soon he trotted past the military field again, where the king's soldiers were still marching. "Remind me never to join the Macedonian army," said Jack.

Annie laughed. "We'd better get Buddy back to the barn before everyone wakes up," she said.

"Okay. Then we'll figure out what to do next," said Jack, "about helping Alexander and stuff."

"And we have to learn a truth about greatness from him, too," said Annie. "Remember our mission?" She held out her hand, reminding Jack about the Ring of Truth.

"Right," said Jack. He'd almost forgotten. "Keep checking that ring to see if it's glowing."

"I am," said Annie. "Don't worry."

The stallion gathered speed and cantered up the road toward the market square. By now, the sellers were setting out their fish and fruits and vegetables.

Jack looked up at the hilltop. King Philip's white mansion caught the fiery light of the rising sun. "We need to take you back to your stall now, Buddy," he said.

The stallion stepped carefully up the pebble path. When they reached the stable area, Jack spied the king and his companions walking toward the riding ring. "Oh, no! They're here already," he said.

"Then let's take Buddy through the stable's back entrance," said Annie. "Hurry!"

"Good idea," said Jack. He shifted his weight. "Turn, Buddy, go right."

The stallion changed direction and headed for the back of the stable. But as they drew closer, Jack saw someone standing in the open doorway.

It was Prince Alexander.

CHAPTER NINE

The Truth

The stallion stopped and neighed at the prince. Alexander stood with his legs apart and his arms crossed. He was not smiling.

"Hi there!" Annie said.

Alexander didn't answer. He glared at Jack and Annie. "I shall have you punished for stealing him," he said. "I have been looking for him everywhere."

"We didn't steal him. We just took him out for a ride," said Jack.

"Why did he let you two ride him?" Alexander asked. "Of all people?"

Jack started to make a comment about Alexander's attitude, but then he made a different decision—he decided to be kind. "Maybe he let us ride him because he knew that *you* are a friend of ours," he said.

The prince looked confused by Jack's answer. "Really?" he asked.

Jack nodded.

"Well, I suppose that could be possible," Alexander said. He cleared his throat and took a deep breath. "So where did he take you?" he asked. The anger had left his voice. Now it was filled with curiosity.

"We just rode through town and down the main road and around the swamps and fields," said Annie. "I wish you'd been with us!" She swung her leg over the horse's back and slid to the ground.

Jack did the same. The stallion neighed and brushed his head against Annie, then Jack. Annie giggled. "That tickles," she said.

"How did you tame him?" Alexander asked.

"We listened to him," said Jack.

"Listened to him?" the prince asked. "What do you mean?"

"It was sort of like . . . we forgot about ourselves and paid total attention to him instead," said Jack.

Alexander watched as Annie and Jack stroked the stallion's mane. "My father vows he will not waste his gold on this horse," he said. "But I . . . I see something very special in him. I believe he is extraordinary."

"He is," said Jack. "He's incredibly loyal."

"And he has a great heart," said Annie.

"I know. I can tell," said Alexander.

"Maybe you could tell your father that you will pay for him yourself," suggested Annie. "Do you get an allowance?"

"I do not know what that means," said Alexander. "But no matter. I doubt that my father would agree to anything I propose. He has no respect for my opinions—or my accomplishments."

"Your father is wrong not to give you respect,"

said Jack, and he meant it. "One day all the history books will call you Alexander the Great."

"Are you mocking me?" Alexander said, scowling.

"No! It's true, I promise," said Jack.

"Believe us," said Annie. "We know."

"But listen," said Jack. "Being great doesn't mean you go around bragging about yourself all the time."

"Don't tell everyone that you are a living Greek god," said Annie, "or that you're going to be master of the universe."

"Or that you are the best athlete in the known world," said Jack. "Just accept that no matter what you can do, you're still a regular human being, a person like everyone else."

"Are you insulting me?" said Alexander.

"No!" said Jack with a smile. "Stop that! We're *all* regular human beings. Why don't you just let yourself be a real person for a change and laugh at yourself? Be okay with making mistakes and looking like a fool."

"Jack's right," said Annie. "Know that sometimes you're great and sometimes you're terrible. You're strong and you're weak."

The prince frowned. "A fool? Terrible? Weak?" he said.

"The truth is this: *nobody's* perfect. Even you," said Jack. "So just accept it."

"You speak nonsense," said Alexander.

"It's called humility," said Jack.

"Humility?" the prince said slowly.

"Jack!" said Annie. "Look!" She held her hand close to Jack's face. The Ring of Truth was glowing as if it were made of fire.

Jack smiled again. "Yes. Humility," he said to the prince. *That* was the secret of greatness that Merlin wanted them to discover on this mission.

"But you cannot expect me to show humility to the world," said Alexander, shaking his head. "No mighty king would ever do that."

"Well, no matter what you have to do to be a mighty king, you can at least have humility inside yourself," said Annie. "And if you do, I promise this horse will trust you."

"There he is!" a gruff voice said.

Jack, Annie, and Alexander turned to see two grooms coming out of the barn. One of the grooms held a whip.

"You were looking for this horse?" Prince Alexander asked sternly. He stepped between the stallion and the grooms.

"The king wants to see him in the ring again, with the others," said the first groom. He moved around Alexander toward the stallion. As the man's shadow fell over Buddy, the stallion snorted loudly and shied away.

Alexander jumped in front of the groom. "Get away from him!" he ordered the man. "Leave him alone!"

The groom stepped back.

"Leave us!" roared Alexander.

The two grooms turned and disappeared back into the barn.

Buddy neighed.

"Shh, my friend, shh," Alexander said softly, stepping toward the stallion. "You mustn't be afraid."

The horse shook out his mane and backed up.

"Alexander, listen to him," Jack whispered.

"Remember . . . humility," whispered Annie.

Alexander stopped and stared into the horse's eyes. The horse stared back at him. The prince slowly held out his hand and stroked the horse's head. Then he spoke softly. "Something frightened you just now," he said, "when the man stepped in front of you. What was it?"

Buddy blinked and lowered his head.

"The . . . shadows?" asked Alexander. The prince held still. Buddy raised his head. He and Alexander stared at each other for a moment.

Then Alexander turned to Jack and Annie. "I listened, and I heard him!" he said in a voice filled with wonder. "He is frightened by shadows. I must remember to always mount him with both of us facing the sun."

Jack and Annie grinned at each other. Jack didn't know if Alexander had really heard the horse's thoughts, but he knew that Alexander and the stallion would be fine together.

"Now you should prove to your father that you can ride him," Annie said to the prince.

Alexander nodded. "Yes," he said, his eyes sparkling. He looked like a different person. "Yes, I will."

"Good," said Jack. "Go stand with the king. We'll take Bucephalus through the barn and release him into the ring."

"Thank you!" said Alexander. He left them and

disappeared around the corner of the barn.

"Come on, Buddy," Jack said.

Jack and Annie led the horse through the barn. Before they reached the entrance to the ring, they stopped. The stallion snorted and dipped his head, and they both rubbed his neck and his nose.

"Please help Alexander, Buddy," Jack said. "He needs a loyal friend. And you need one, too."

"We love you," Annie said. "Don't forget that."

A groom appeared at the stable doorway. "Bucephalus!" he shouted.

Jack and Annie reluctantly pulled away from the stallion. "Be great, Bucephalus!" said Jack, his voice cracking.

Bucephalus looked at them with soft eyes. Then he walked with the groom out of the barn, into the riding ring.

"Come on!" said Annie. "Let's go watch!"

Jack and Annie hurried to the back door of the stable. They shot outside into the sunlight and ran around the building to the riding ring.

The king, his companions, and Aristotle were

lined up at the fence. Prince Alexander stood with his father. All eyes were on the black stallion as he trotted around the ring, tossing his head and snorting.

"Good morning!" Aristotle called to Jack and Annie. They ran to join him.

"The king asked about you last night and this morning," he said in a soft voice. "What have you been doing?"

"Training them," Annie said breathlessly.

"Training who?" the philosopher asked.

"The stallion," said Annie.

"The prince," said Jack.

Aristotle raised his eyebrows, but before he could speak, the king's voice rang out. "Come back, you fool!"

Jack, Annie, and Aristotle all looked at the ring.

Prince Alexander had hopped over the fence. He was heading toward the black stallion.

CHAPTER TEN

A Place of Honor

"Alexander! Do not try to ride him!" King Philip yelled at the prince. "Do not be a fool!"

Alexander ran around the ring. Soon he was running alongside Bucephalus. When the stallion was facing the sun, Alexander vaulted onto his back.

Bucephalus broke into a canter. Horse and boy moved together perfectly around and around the riding ring.

The King's Companions clapped and cheered.

Jack, Annie, and Aristotle joined them. King Philip stared in amazement.

The prince raised his right arm in the air. He looked over at Jack and Annie and shouted with victory.

Laughing, they both gave him a thumbs-up.

"You're great, too, Buddy!" Annie shouted.

The horse neighed.

The king himself then broke into applause. He was smiling with pride at Alexander.

"How amazing!" said Aristotle. "That horse will have the highest place of honor as the prince's horse now."

"Cool," said Jack. He sighed, and then looked at Annie. "Are you ready to go home?"

"Ready," she said with a grin.

"Must you leave now?" said Aristotle. "I know King Philip plans to invite you to stay in the Royal House. Will you not stay and help me educate Alexander?"

"No. We have to go back to our parents," said

Annie. "Pretty soon we'll start missing them."

"Don't worry," Jack said. "You'll do a good job with Alexander. All the world will say that someday."

"Just get him to work on the idea of humility," said Annie.

"Humility?" asked the philosopher.

"Yes," said Jack. "Tell him that one of the secrets of greatness is humility. He's great enough that he can afford to have humility."

"Even if only you and he and Bucephalus know it," added Annie.

"I will remember," said the philosopher.

"Thanks for all your help," said Jack.

"Tell Alexander good-bye for us, please," said Annie.

Jack and Annie stepped away from the fence and headed toward the hill path. They crunched over the pebbles, down to the square. Then they started down the main road, away from town.

They passed the field where the warriors were still marching. They passed the shepherd, the sheep, the goat herder, the goats, and the farmer plowing with the ox. They passed the rocky meadows dotted with cows, until they came to the olive grove. They were about to head between the trees when they heard galloping behind them.

They turned and saw Prince Alexander thundering toward them on the back of Bucephalus. Clouds of dust billowed behind the horse.

"Jack and Annie!" Alexander cried. He brought Bucephalus to a halt.

The stallion shook out his mane, then dipped his head and whinnied. Jack and Annie rubbed his muzzle. "Hey, you," said Jack. "It's good to see you again!"

The prince was out of breath. "You . . . you did not say good-bye!" he said.

"Sorry!" said Jack.

"We have to get home now," said Annie.

"You did a great job!" said Jack.

"You really did!" said Annie. "You and Bucephalus were made for each other!"

"My father thinks so, too," said Alexander, smiling broadly. "After he saw me ride today, he said, 'My son, you had better find a larger kingdom, because mine will not be big enough for you!'"

"Oh, brother," Jack said, "so much for humility."

Surprisingly, Alexander laughed. "Thank you for everything you did for me," he said.

"You're welcome," said Annie. "Have a good life with Bucephalus."

"I will. Jack and Annie, you make me want to travel all over the world with him," said Alexander. "You make me want to know about all things—like koala bears and kangaroos."

"That's great," said Annie.

"You make me want to surround myself with thinkers and scientists and travelers," said Alexander.

"Cool," said Jack.

"You make me want to sing my song to the four quarters of the earth!" shouted Alexander.

Jack smiled. "Do that. Go sing your song," he said.

"I will! Farewell, my friends!" said the prince. "We are going back to inspect my army now!" He and Bucephalus turned around and took off down the dusty road.

"Give those army guys a rest, why don't you?" yelled Annie.

Jack laughed. "Come on," he said.

He and Annie ran through the olive grove to the rope ladder. They climbed up into the tree house and looked out the window. In the distance the prince and his magnificent horse were dashing up the dirt road.

"I almost expect them to take off and soar into the sky," said Annie. "At least that's what riding Buddy felt like to me."

Jack's heart was heavy as they watched Alexander and Bucephalus disappear into a cloud of dust lit by the morning sun. "Good-bye, Buddy," he said.

"Bye, Buddy," Annie echoed.

Jack sighed. "Well, the good news is Buddy will have a place of honor for life."

"And Alexander will have a friend for life," said Annie.

Jack picked up their Pennsylvania book from the corner of the tree house. He pointed to a picture of the Frog Creek woods. "I wish we could go home!"

The wind started to blow.

The tree house started to spin.

It spun faster and faster.

Then everything was still.

Absolutely still.

✽ ◊ ✽

A soft summer breeze blew through the tree house window. Jack and Annie were wearing their own clothes again.

"Mission accomplished," said Jack.

"I'd better leave the ring here," said Annie. She pulled the Ring of Truth off her finger and carefully placed it on the floor in a patch of sunlight. Jack put the bottle of magic mist and the book about Macedonia beside the ring.

"Good. Let's go," said Annie.

"Wait—how can we give our secret of greatness a place of honor?" Jack asked.

Annie shrugged. "We could just write it down," she said.

"I guess that'll work," said Jack. He carefully tore one of the last pieces of paper out of his notebook and wrote in large letters:

HUMILITY

Jack slipped the paper under the Ring of Truth. Maybe it was just the morning light, but the ring seemed to glow brighter as it lay on the paper.

Jack pulled on his backpack. "Ready?" he asked.

"Yep," said Annie. "Let's go sing our song to the four quarters of the earth."

"Why not?" said Jack.

Jack and Annie went down the ladder. Then they walked together through the dappled sunshine. The air smelled of summer. Crows called out to each other.

"It feels good to be home," said Annie.

"No kidding," said Jack.

They came to the edge of the Frog Creek woods and crossed the street and started up the sidewalk.

"I'm so thirsty," said Jack.

"Me too," said Annie. "Hey, we can have some of Dad's lemonade."

"Cool," said Jack.

"I'm really glad Dad's our father instead of King Philip the Second of Macedonia," said Annie.

"Tell Dad that," said Jack.

"Yeah, I will," said Annie. "It'll totally confuse him." They both laughed, and then took off running for home.

Author's Note

Many historians praise Alexander the Great for being one of the most successful military leaders of all time. He led his men into battle with intelligence and courage and created the biggest empire the world had ever seen. Alexander had great curiosity about the world and a thirst for knowledge. On his expeditions he took along builders, scientists, writers, and artists.

While some historians criticize Alexander for having been a ruthless conqueror, all agree he had a loving devotion to his warhorse, Bucephalus. Bucephalus is one of the most famous horses of all time. Historians believe he was taken captive in Thessaly and was probably four years old when he was brought to Macedonia.

Bucephalus was wild when Prince Alexander first laid eyes on him. The prince managed to tame and mount him before a crowd that included his father, King Philip II. Thereafter, the horse became the magnificent and beloved warhorse of Alexander the Great.

For my story, I imagined that Bucephalus was a magnificent horse before he met Alexander, and that perhaps something had happened in his past to make him resist new riders. . . .

To find out more about horses that did heroic deeds, read the Magic Tree House Fact Tracker: *Horse Heroes*!

You'll love finding out the facts
behind the fiction in

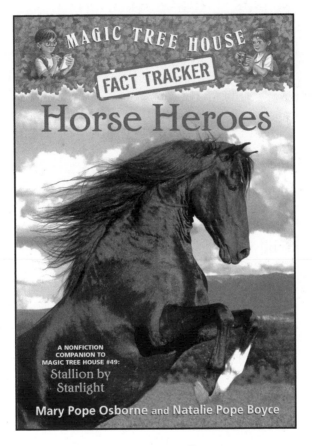

Turn the page to read an excerpt.

Horses are measured in <u>hands</u>. A hand is four inches. Fifteen hands high is sixty inches tall from the ground to the top of the withers. (That's five feet tall.)

In the time of knights and castles, knights rode a type of warhorse called a *destrier* (DES-tree-er). Destriers weighed twice as much as other horses. They had extra strength to carry knights wearing heavy armor into battle.

Farmers wanted large horses for farmwork. Many of the biggest horses today come from hundreds of years of careful breeding. The largest, tallest, and strongest workhorse is the *Shire* horse. The English have been breeding Shires for 800 years. They can weigh more than 2,200 pounds and be over twenty hands high!

Among the fastest horses today are Thoroughbreds. Thoroughbreds are relatives of Arabians. The English began breeding them for racing in the 1600s. They are still racing today. These tall, light horses usually reach speeds of about forty miles an hour. There are millions of Thoroughbreds all over the world.

Word	Meaning
mare	female horse
stallion	male horse
foal	horse under one year old
pony	small horse
filly	young female horse
colt	young male horse

The Tea Horse Road

The Tea Horse Road wasn't actually a road. It was a series of paths covering almost 1,400 miles from China to Tibet. Beginning about a thousand years ago, men, women, and mules hauled millions of pounds of tea from China to trade for Tibetan horses. The trails were very dangerous. The workers faced raging rivers, steep valleys, rain, snow, and mountain passes 17,000 feet high. Some carried loads of over 300 pounds on their backs.

When they got to Tibet, tea was traded for horses. The Tibetans bred strong, fine horses. The Chinese needed them to fight off hordes of nomad raiders. At certain times as many as 25,000 horses a year arrived in China from Tibet!

The trade in horses continued until the end of the 1800s. After that, the Chinese traded tea for goods like gold, medicine, silver, and cloth. Traffic on the trails didn't stop until 1949. Today much of the trail has disappeared and is covered with weeds or concrete highways.

Coming in July 2013!

Jack and Annie find out about the greatest magician who ever lived: Harry Houdini!

Learn how to do your own magic tricks with Jack and Annie!